The Scenic Route

A Collection of Inspirational Quotes

Written by May Ewald

Best wishes,
May E Ewald

Copyright © 2005 by May Ewald. 26150-EWAL
Library of Congress: 2004097938
ISBN: Softcover   1-4134-6599-4
           Hardcover   1-4134-6600-1

All rights reserved. No part of this book may be reproduced or transmitted in any form or by any means, electronic or mechanical, including photocopying, recording, or by any information storage and retrieval system, without permission in writing from the copyright owner.

This book was printed in the United States of America.

Photo Credits

May Ewald—pgs. 4, 12, 14, 22, 40, 48, 52, 54, 64, 66
Ashley Gregory—pgs. 24, 60
Spring Ligi—pgs. 6, 16, 21, 26, 30, 33, 34, 36, 38, 42, 44, 46, 50, 56, 59, 62
Bob Updegrove—cover, pgs. 9, 10, 18
Anonymous—pg. 29

To order additional copies of this book, contact:
Xlibris Corporation
1-888-795-4274
www.Xlibris.com
Orders@Xlibris.com

*Many thanks to Spring Ligi,
Bob Updegrove, and Ashley Gregory for the
beautiful pictures they contributed to this book.
Thanks also to Mom and Dad, Grandma and
Grandpa Ewald, and Steve Ligi for their
help and support.*

*If given a choice to take the highway
or back roads, choose the scenic route.*

*You are here to make a difference.
The question is not why but how.*

Believe in yourself . . .
Believe in anything worth fighting for . . .
Believe because you can.

Assume nothing;
    Life consists of endless possibilities.

*The only limits you face
are the ones you have created.*

There's more than one solution to every problem.

*When your thoughts
conflict with emotions,
follow your heart.*

Why step in another's footprints when you can make your own?

If you have made the wrong decision, choose again.

*How easy it is to complicate
the simplicity of life.*

*Sometimes it's best
to say nothing at all.*

You influence everyone you meet;
you have the power to
help or hurt,
ignore or inspire,
encourage or criticize.

Don't hold back from others
for fear they will not always be
in your life. It is when you
walk away with tears in your eyes
that you have truly lived.

*Forgiveness enables
you to let go of the hurt
caused by others.*

Beyond the disguise of
outside appearances lies the
beauty of every spirit.

Do not envy another's life.
Find the value inside yourself.

Those who have enough have it all.

What's important to you?
Prioritize your life.

*Passion
wakes up the soul!*

*Each day reveals a new lesson
for those willing to learn.*

Tomorrow is determined by how you live today.

*Time is precious to those
who know there is never enough.*

The most important things in life are always worth the wait.

Success is the result of persevering through every failure.

It takes one hundred and ten percent effort to reach your potential.

Expect too much, you'll be disappointed.
Expect too little, you'll never improve.
Expect just enough to be content
with your best.

A hero steps up to the plate
when no one else will.

Be courageous—face your fears.

*Never underestimate
how much you can endure.*

When faced with hardship remember that nothing in this world is permanent.

Change provides the opportunity to view life from a new perspective.

*Learn from mistakes,
Overcome fears,
Work toward success,
Leave no regrets.*

*In the end,
love is
enough.*